MAX CHAMPION AND THE GREAT RACE CAR ROBBERY

Also by Alexander McCall Smith

Freddie Mole, Lion Tamer

*

Explosive Adventures
Marvellous Mix-Ups

MAX CHAMPION AND THE GREAT RACE CAR ROBBERY

ALEXANDER McCALL SMITH
ILLUSTRATED BY KATE HINDLEY

BLOOMSBURY
CHILDREN'S BOOKS
LONDON OXFORD NEW YORK NEW DELHI SYDNEY

BLOOMSBURY CHILDREN'S BOOKS
Bloomsbury Publishing Plc
50 Bedford Square, London, WC1B 3DP, UK

BLOOMSBURY, BLOOMSBURY CHILDREN'S BOOKS and the Diana logo
are trademarks of Bloomsbury Publishing Plc

First published in Great Britain in April 2018 by Bloomsbury Publishing Plc

Text copyright © Alexander McCall Smith, 2018
Illustrations copyright © Kate Hindley, 2018

Alexander McCall Smith has asserted his right under the Copyright, Designs
and Patents Act, 1988, to be identified as Author of this work

A catalogue record for this book is available from the British Library

ISBN: HB: 978-1-4088-8613-7; PB: 978-1-4088-8612-0;
eBook: 978-1-4088-8611-3

2 4 6 8 10 9 7 5 3 1

Typeset by RefineCatch Limited, Bungay, Suffolk
Printed and bound in Great Britain by CPI Group (UK) Ltd, Croydon CR0 4YY

To find out more about our authors and books visit www.bloomsbury.com
and sign up for our newsletters

This book is for Harry and Ruaridh

This is the story of Max Champion and a great thing he did. Max is the hero of this tale because that is what he was, by nature and by deed — a hero.

His full name was Max George Henry William Champion, but nobody needs that many names and so he was simply called Max. He lived with his mother, who was called Molly, and his grandfather, Augustus Monty Champion, known as Gus.

Their home was at the end of a track on the edge of town. It was not a large house – in fact, it was rather small, only having three tiny rooms and an outside shack. This meant there was a bedroom for Molly, one for Max and a room that was used for everything else, including cooking and washing. Baths were taken in a tin tub behind a curtain; there was no hot tap, and so water was heated on the stove before being poured into the tub. It was all rather simple, but it was a comfortable tub and nobody complained.

Grandfather Gus lived in a small shed in the back yard. Max had offered him his room and said that he would take the shed

instead, but Grandfather Gus simply shook his head and said he would not hear of it.

"I slept in all sorts of places in my younger days," he said. "I've slept in tents and igloos. I've slept in haystacks and caves. I don't mind a shed one little bit – in fact, I think this is one of the most comfortable places I've ever slept in my life!"

The Champion family did not have much money. Grandfather Gus had a small garage, where he had worked for as long as anybody could remember. This garage was right next to the house, which meant he did not have far to walk to get to work. It was always surrounded by the old cars Gus fixed. These cars belonged to people who could not afford newer cars, and it was only through Gus's efforts that they were kept going at all.

"If only I could buy better tools," said Gus. "Then I could fix some of the more modern cars too." He sighed. It was not easy fixing these old cars, but it was his work and he did it as cheerfully as he could. The Champion family was not the sort of family who complained about anything – they made do with what they had.

Everybody had to earn what money they could – even Max, who had a part-time job when he was not at school. Molly, his mother, worked as a sandwich-maker in a nearby town; Max's job was to cut people's lawns. For this, he had an old lawnmower that just about worked, although it needed a lot of pushing and shoving to do anything very much. On the afternoons that he cut grass, he would come home completely exhausted by all the effort, hardly finding the energy needed to eat the dinner his mother had prepared for him.

"I'm sorry you have to work so hard, Max," his mother said. "Other boys have time to play – I wish you did."

Max told her not to worry about him. "I'm doing fine, Mum," he said. "I like my work – I really do."

She knew he was being kind and he was

just thinking of her feelings. That made her proud: her son was a hard worker and always shared what he earned. Even so, it was difficult to make ends meet, and at the end of each week there was never much money left in the jar in the kitchen where they all put their earnings.

On Saturday mornings, before he went off to mow lawns, Max helped his grandfather in the garage. He was not allowed to do the difficult things that only a mechanic could do, but he could help in other ways. He could unscrew the nuts that let dirty oil drain out of engines. He could do that quite easily, and could collect the old oil in deep trays. He could also change the rubber blades on wind-screen wipers, fill a cooling system with water and check the air pressure in tyres. All these could be done while Grandfather Gus was attending to the more complicated issues of brakes and lights and gearboxes.

Another thing Max could do was clean cars. Many of the vehicles that were brought to the garage for repair were very dirty, and needed to be thoroughly washed before being returned to their owners. Max liked this job, as there was a high-pressure hose he could use to remove layers of grime as easily as if it were icing on a cake.

"Be careful with that thing," warned Gus. "It's very powerful. Make sure that you don't damage the cars."

Max was careful, and after he had removed the outer layers of dirt, he would often complete the job with a bucket of warm water, some soap and a cloth. In this way he would coax the last of the dirt off the car's bodywork. Then he would polish so hard that the car would end up gleaming and looking almost as

good as new. The owners of these cars would marvel at the transformation.

"You've made my poor old car look brand new," exclaimed one of them. "Max – you're a real hero, you know!"

Max was modest. "I'm glad you like it," he said.

It was while he was cleaning a car one Saturday morning that he made his discovery. He was working in the garage with his mother, who sometimes stood in for Gus if he was called away to deal with a breakdown. She was not a trained mechanic, but she had picked up a lot over the years and could fix most simple things that went wrong. That morning a car had been brought in by its owner, a farmer, who apologised for its dirty state. He had meant to clean it before he brought it in to be fixed, but had been too busy getting his pigs and sheep ready for market.

"Don't worry," said Molly. "My son is pretty good at washing and polishing. I've never known a car that he can't sort out, given the chance."

Max beamed with pleasure at the compliment. He was pleased that his mother was proud of him. And so he set to work on the car, which was so covered in mud that it was hard to tell what colour it was underneath. It could have been blue, but then it could equally well have been red or white, or even some shade in-between.

Max applied the high-pressure hose to the back of the car, to remove the worst of the mud before he started to scrub the bodywork with his cloth. And that is when he saw it: underneath the grime was a line of raised metal lettering.

This car was an unusual shape, and Max was keen to discover what make it was. The lettering, he thought, would give him the answer.

Slowly he uncovered the half-hidden letters. First there came a C, then an H, and after that an A. Now he was interested: he had not heard of a car whose

name began with those letters, and he was keen to find out what followed. It was an M, and then, immediately after that, a P. At last it was fully uncovered: *Champion*.

Max stood back and scratched his head. *Champion?* Why would a car have that name on it – which happened to be their family name? He was puzzled, and could think of no reason to explain this strange discovery.

His mother was working on a tractor that needed new brakes, and was at a tricky stage of the repair.

"I'm busy," she said, when Max asked her to come and see what he had found. "Later on, please, Max."

"But, Mum," protested Max, "there's a car over there with our name on it."

Molly stood up straight, wiping her hands on her overalls. "Did you say *our name*?" she asked.

"Yes," said Max. "It says *Champion*."

"I think I should take a look at this," said Molly, as she made her way to the other side of the garage.

Bending down to examine the lettering,

Max's mother gasped in surprise. She turned to Max, a broad smile on her face. "Do you realise who made this car, Max?" she asked.

Max shook his head.

Molly's smile became even broader. "Grandfather Gus," she said proudly. "He made it."

~ 2 ~

It took Max a few moments to grasp what his mother had said.

"Grandfather Gus?" he asked. "Do you mean *he* made this car ... himself?"

Molly pointed to the front of the car. "I think we should take a look inside," she suggested. "Come with me." And with that, she opened one of the car doors, gesturing for Max to slip in beside her.

If the car had been dirty outside, inside

16

it was a different story. The farmer who owned it had been careful to keep it clean, and there was hardly a speck of dust on the instrument panel or the steering wheel.

"It's beautiful," said Max, feeling the soft leather of the seats. "This is a really nice car, Mum."

Molly looked proud. "It is, isn't it? And there are very few of these around, Max – maybe ten, maybe not quite that many. You never see them on the roads these days."

There was so much Max wanted to ask his mother, that he did not know where to start. But Molly settled that question.

"Would you like to hear the whole story?" she asked. "I've been meaning to tell you, but I never got around to it."

They sat in the front seats of the car, just the two of them, which was a good place to hear a story, as it was warm and comfortable.

"Well," began Molly, "this is how it starts …"

Max closed his eyes. He had always done that when he was told a story, as it somehow made it easier for him to picture what was going on.

"Your grandfather," said Molly, "used to have a factory. It was not a very big factory – not much more than a rather long shed, in fact. He bought it very cheaply because the man who used to own it had stopped making things. He used to make metal spoons for marmalade jars, and suddenly everybody stopped using them and bought plastic ones instead. So he sold the factory to your grandfather for next to nothing. He gave him the machines as well – they could cut metal

and mould it into various shapes, and
that, I suppose, is why your grandfather
thought he might make a car – just to see
how things worked.

"Now, most of us would not be much
good at making a car, but your grandfather, Max, is different. He's a type of
genius, you know – an inventor! You
didn't know that, did you?"

Max shook his head. Grandfather Gus
was just ... well, he was just Grandfather
Gus: it had never occurred to Max that he
might have been able to invent things.

"There he was with his factory," continued Molly. "And he decided to make a
car from the ground upwards. So, he

bought some wheels from somewhere or other, and then he built the chassis – that's the car's skeleton, you know – and then he worked out how to make an engine, from bits and pieces he bought here and there. And then ..." Max's mother paused, "... it worked. The car actually started."

Max opened his eyes and stared at his mother in astonishment. "It started?" he asked. "And then it actually ..."

His mother nodded. "It ran as sweetly as a bee," she said. "So he put his name on the back and began to make another one, and another one after that."

"What did he do with them?" asked Max.

"He sold them," said Molly. "There were plenty of people who wanted a car like that, and they were happy to buy one. In fact, he had a waiting list for Champion cars."

Max shook his head in wonderment. "I had no idea," he said.

"Your grandfather's a very modest man," said Molly. "He's never been the type to boast. So he didn't go around talking about how good his cars were. But he did write everything down in his Ideas Book."

"Ideas Book?" asked Max.

"Yes," replied Molly. "That's where he sketched out the plans for his cars. There

were hundreds of drawings in it — a real treasure trove of ideas."

Now Molly looked sad, and Max knew that the story was not going to end well.

"Have you heard of a man called Grabber?" she asked.

Max shook his head.

"This Mr Grabber," said Molly, "saw

that your grandfather was doing well, and he did not like it. He had his own car factory. His cars were not much use, to tell the truth. He cut corners when he made them — saving money, even on things like brakes. But he still wanted to do better than anybody else, and so he cooked up a scheme."

Max waited.

"And this scheme," she continued, "was to somehow stop your grandfather from making his cars."

"How did he do that?" asked Max.

"It was complicated," explained his mother. "But Mr Grabber found out that Grandfather Gus had borrowed money from a bank to buy some new machinery. Now, the bank that lent him the money was not big at all — in fact, it was very small — and so Mr Grabber was able to buy the bank itself, lock, stock and barrel. Then, once he owned it, he simply said to Grandfather Gus that he had to pay the money back immediately."

Max's face fell. "And he couldn't?"

Molly shook her head. "I'm afraid he couldn't. So Mr Grabber was able to move in and take over his business. He took the factory and everything inside it. He wasn't allowed to take Grandfather Gus's papers, but he did that nonetheless. He took the Ideas Book."

Max drew in his breath. "With all the plans? With all the ideas?"

His mother nodded sadly. "Yes, he stole the Ideas Book."

Max wondered why his grandfather did not go to the police, and Molly explained to him that he had no proof Mr Grabber had taken the book. So the police were unable to do anything.

"After that," Molly said, "Grandfather Gus more or less gave up. He had just enough money to buy the garage, and since then he has spent the rest of his time working here. He does not make much money, as you know, but he helps lots of people keep their cars going.

He is proud of that."

Max waited for more, but it seemed this was the end of the story. What he had heard made him feel sad and angry – at the same time. It seemed so unfair that Grandfather Gus should have lost everything, and it seemed so wrong that Mr Grabber should have got away with it. He wondered about Mr Grabber – was he still around? Was he still getting away with it? This is what he now asked his mother.

"Oh, the Grabbers are still with us," said Molly. "There are two of them now – Mr Grabber himself and his son, Pablo Grabber. He's about the same age as you are, and he's every bit as nasty as his father."

"Where do they live?" asked Max.

"Not far away," said his mother. "You sometimes see them going past in their big car. They still make cars – and race them too. Just like your grandfather did."

Max had not heard that before. "So Grandfather Gus was a racing driver?" he asked.

"Yes," said his mother. "He took part in those long road races – rallies – where they drive ordinary cars. He was very good at it." She paused. "He often beat the Grabbers, which they didn't like one little bit. People like that want to come first in everything."

"Isn't there anything we can do?" he asked.

"I'm afraid not," said Molly. "But, there we are. We should just get on with our lives as best we can — and I think we're doing that, don't you?"

Max nodded. He was glad that he was a member of a happy family, even if they did not have much money and had to scrape around a bit to get by. Grandfather Gus had often told him that the most important thing in life was happiness – the happiness you feel inside you – and his mother had said much the same thing. Max thought they were both right, although sometimes there were things that could make you feel quite unhappy – as the story he had just heard from his mother had done.

Molly opened the car door for her son to get out. "I think we should get on with our work," she said. Then she added,

"You should ask your grandfather about his days as a car maker. It's an amazing story."

"Yes," said Max. "I'd like to hear it."

~ 3 ~

He spoke to Grandfather Gus that very evening, seated around the small wood stove that the old man had in his shack. At night this was what kept the shack warm, although sometimes, when it was very cold outside, small patches of ice would form on the inside of the windows. This did not worry Grandfather Gus too much, as he said that it was not good for you to be too hot.

Max told him about how he had discovered the car.

"So you found an old Champion," said Grandfather Gus with a smile. "That's quite a thing to discover, Max – there aren't many of those around these days."

"It was very well kept inside," said Max. "The wood panels were polished and all the steel gleamed like new."

Grandfather Gus nodded. "They were great cars, those Champions," he said. "Very pretty machines. Do you know they could go at one hundred miles an hour, sometimes more?"

"That's very fast," said Max.

"And they were as comfortable as a

living-room sofa," went on Grandfather Gus. "Even on bumpy roads, your skeleton never complained. It was like riding on air, people said. That was the suspension I designed – it was very special." He paused, as if about to reveal a secret. "And you know something, Max? That suspension *was* really special – it was the only suspension in the world, as far as I know, that used marshmallow. Would you believe that?"

Max looked astonished. He knew that marshmallow was spongy, sweet stuff that quickly melted in your mouth, but he had never heard of it being used to make suspension for cars.

Grandfather Gus looked dreamy. "Ah," he said, "I remember some of the drives I had in one of the first Champions I made. She was a lovely car, she was. I gave her a name, Arabella, and I used her for years. I was making other Champions for people in those days, but I always kept that one as my personal car."

"You must have loved her," said Max.

"Yes," said Grandfather Gus. "I did. And I had some amazing adventures in her. Did I ever tell you about those?"

Max shook his head. "No, but I'd love to hear them."

Grandfather Gus put another log in the stove and patted the seat beside him.

"In that case, come and sit down here beside me, and I'll get out my photograph album and show you pictures of some of the things Arabella and I got up to in those days."

Seated next to his grandfather, Max looked at the dusty album with its collection of old photographs. On the first page there was a large picture of what Max now recognised as a Champion. It was a large green car with the number five painted on its side, and Grandfather Gus, looking much younger, was standing proudly beside it.

"There we are just before setting off

for India," said Grandfather Gus. "Did I ever tell you we went on a great car rally all the way to India?'

Max was astonished. "That must have taken ages," he said.

"Yes it did," said Grandfather Gus. "There were fifty cars involved, you know, and we were all trying to get to India as quickly as possible. But it took two months, as I recall. And we were driving every day – mile after mile every day. I had somebody to read the maps for me, of course."

He turned the page to show Max the next photograph. "Here we are in France," he said. "Just before we went over the Alps. We were in first place at that stage – way ahead of everyone else."

He turned another page. Now he was in Turkey, parked outside a cafe in Istanbul, holding a large glass of fizzy drink and smiling at the camera.

"That drink was sherbet," said Grandfather Gus. "It was sweet and delicious, and it tickled the inside of your nose as you drank it."

In the next photograph they were on a narrow mountain road. It made Max's stomach turn just to look at the drop at the edge of the road – it went down and down, until it reached a river at the bottom of a gorge. The river was so far down below that it was no more than a thin silver ribbon, but Max knew that if the car fell off the side of the road it would not take long for it to plummet all the way to the bottom.

"That was pretty dangerous," said Grandfather Gus, pointing to the drop. "One little mistake and, oh dear, we wouldn't have stood much of a chance."

Max did not like to think of it. "Well, you made it," he said. "And that's what counts."

"We were still in first place at that point," said Grandfather Gus. "But that was to change once we reached India." He looked dejected. "I still feel sad about what happened."

Max waited for him to explain.

"Here we are," he said, turning the page to reveal the next photograph. "Broken down."

It was a sad picture. A cloud of steam was coming from Arabella's engine, while Grandfather Gus and his map reader stood by helplessly.

"It just suddenly exploded," said Grandfather Gus. "We were in the middle of India then, and only a few hundred miles from the finishing line."

"You must have been so disappointed," said Max. "Just when everything was going so well, that happened."

Grandfather Gus shook his head sadly. "Yes," he said. "And do you know something, Max? I think it was sabotage."

Max frowned. He had heard the word before, but was not quite sure what it meant. But seeing his expression, Grandfather Gus went on to say, "I think that one of the other competitors put something in our fuel. There were signs that the fuel inlet had been tampered with, and that would explain why the engine exploded."

Max was outraged. "Did you know who it was?" he asked. "Did you report them?"

Grandfather Gus sighed. "I had a good idea who it was," he said. "But I didn't have any proof."

Max waited for him to say who it was, and when the answer came he was not altogether surprised.

"There's a man called Adolphus Grabber," said Grandfather Gus. "He was one of the other entrants. He was racing one of his own cars – a car called the Grabber Guzzler, because it used so much fuel. It was really a pretty horrible car, actually, but he was very proud of it and he wanted to win at all costs. I think he was the person who sabotaged my beautiful Arabella."

"So what happened next?" asked Max.

"Well," said Grandfather Gus, "there was not much I could do. We were in the middle of nowhere with a car that was not going anywhere. The nearest garage was miles away and poor old Arabella simply wouldn't budge. And not only that – we had very little water with us, and next to no food."

He smiled at Max.

"But just when things were looking

very grim, something turned up – as it often does."

"A towing truck?" asked Max.

Grandfather Gus laughed. "No, not that, but something every bit as useful. Do you think you can guess?"

Max tried, but could not think of anything.

"An elephant," said Grandfather Gus at last. "It was one of those working elephants that they have in India – you know, the ones who help carry great trees in the forest, once they've cut them down."

"He came along all by himself?" asked Max.

"No," said Grandfather Gus. "He had his keeper with him. They call those people *mahouts*. And this one was riding along on top of the elephant, when he came round the corner and saw us by the side of the road.

"He was a very kind man," continued Grandfather Gus. "When he saw that Arabella was broken down, he offered to tow us with his elephant. He had a thick rope with him and it did not take him long to tie one end to Arabella and the other to his elephant. Then the elephant started to walk, while I sat at the wheel of the car to steer. It was no effort for such a strong creature – he hardly felt the load at all."

"You were very lucky," said Max.

"I know that," said Grandfather Gus. "And it was a great deal of fun as well. He towed us for two days, all the way to the finishing line in Delhi. And although we came last in the rally, there was still a great crowd waiting to cheer us over the line. When they saw us arriving under elephant power, they cheered and cheered. They brought garlands of flowers for all of us – and for the elephant too – and they let off fire-works to mark our arrival. It was spectacular."

Max could imagine the scene, but there was something he wanted to

know. "Who won in the end?" he asked. "It wasn't ..."

He did not finish his question. "I'm afraid it was," answered Grandfather Gus. "Adolphus Grabber won, in his Grabber Guzzler."

Max looked down at the floor. He felt miserable, even just hearing about this – how much worse must poor Grandfather Gus have felt?

"But, don't worry," said his grandfather. "It doesn't matter too much who wins a race – what really matters is that you enjoy it, and that you play fair. If everybody plays fair, then everybody has a good time."

Max looked at the picture of the car.

"What happened to Arabella?" he asked. "Did she stay in India?"

"Yes," said Grandfather Gus. "I couldn't fix her there, and so I had to leave her. It broke my heart, but there was not much else I could do. I have no idea what happened to her, but I suspect that she was broken up for spare parts."

Max snuggled up to his grandfather. He was the wisest, nicest grandfather anybody could possibly wish for, Max thought, and yet he had been so unfairly treated by Mr Grabber. Sometimes the world seemed so unfair: good people were tricked or bullied by bad people, and the bad people seemed to get away with it. If only he could do some-thing about it, he said to himself. But then he thought: *What can I possibly do?* And the answer, it seemed to him, was: *Not much.*

~ 4 ~

The following week was an important week for the town in which Max lived. Although not very much happened there normally, there was one day in the year when the whole place came alive. This was the day of the town sports, when everybody joined in races and tug-of-war competitions and high jump – and everything else that you find on a typical sports day. At the end of the day, prizes were awarded to the winners, and this was followed by a dance in the town hall. It was a day that everybody looked forward to, even if they could not run very fast, nor pull all that hard in the tug-of-war, nor even jump very high in the high jump.

Max liked running. He was in a running team at school, and he had spent some time training for the town sports, in which he would be entering the boys' mile event and the long jump. He was also a member of a team that was hoping to do well in the relay race.

Grandfather Gus always attended the town sports. For most of the time he just watched, but there was one event he always entered — the grandfathers' weightlifting competition — and the previous year he had come third and won a large bronze medal. He was very proud of this medal and he hoped that this year he might win something again.

"You never know," he said to Max.

When the time came to line up for the relay race, Max and his three teammates made their way to their various positions around the track. The way a relay race works is that the first member of the team sets off and, after running all the way around the track, hands a baton over to the second runner. That person then completes his or her circuit before handing over the baton, and so on, until it is the last member of the team who crosses the finishing line. Max, who was the fastest member of the four of them, would be that last runner.

Max was excited. There were five teams competing in the race, but he thought his team had a good chance of winning. As he stood in place, watching the first of the runners set off, he noticed something that made him catch his breath. One of the runners, a boy of about Max's age who was standing next to him, had his name emblazoned on the front of his shirt: *Pablo Grabber*.

Max wondered whether he had misread the name, but another glance showed him he had not. And at that precise moment, Pablo Grabber looked back in his direction and gave him a sickly smile.

"Have you done this before?" Pablo asked him.

Max pulled himself together. At least Pablo was speaking to him politely, and deserved an answer. "Yes," he said. "I ran in the relay race last year."

Pablo nodded. "I've won the last ten races I've entered," he said, casually. "Every one of them."

Max was surprised that anybody could be so boastful, but he tried not to show what he felt. "Well done," he said.

"Ten races. And this one will be the eleventh."

Max looked at him in astonishment. How could he possibly know that he was going to win this race?

Pablo smiled again. "Sorry about that," he said. "But perhaps you'll come second — if you're lucky."

"We'll see about that," muttered Max, keeping his voice down. Pablo did not hear this, and continued to stretch and run up and down on the spot as he waited for the baton to do its rounds.

At last the third runners were approaching the line where the fourth and final runners were poised, ready to go. Max found himself crouched next to Pablo, but he tried to avoid looking at the annoying and boastful boy. His eyes were fixed firmly on the track ahead, and when his teammate came up behind him, the baton held out to be passed on, Max was off in a great burst of speed.

He did not see Pablo – nobody saw him, because cheats are often very careful to make sure that nobody sees them cheating. So nobody saw Pablo put his leg out just as Max began to run, and nobody saw how Pablo's leg brought Max down on the track, a hard, grazing, painful fall right at the very beginning of the lap.

As he fell, Max saw Pablo shoot past him. And as Max picked himself up, gingerly testing to see that no bones were broken, he saw Pablo speeding down the track, at the head of the other contestants. It was too late for Max to rejoin the race, as the others were now so far ahead. Even if he had been wearing jet-propelled shoes, he would not have been able to catch them up.

Pablo won, crossing the finishing line well ahead of the others. As he did so, he raised his arms in triumph, and then gave himself a good round of applause. Soon he was joined by a large man wearing a white suit. This man seemed very pleased with Pablo's performance, patting him on the back and congratulating him in a loud voice. From where he was standing – close to the place where he had been tripped up – Max was able to hear what was being said.

"Well done, son," shouted the man in the white suit. "That showed them!"

So that's Mr Grabber, thought Max. He took a good look at his face; it was a mean face, the face of a person who would stop at nothing to get his way. It was a greedy face too – the face of one who wanted everything he could possibly have, leaving little for anyone else.

Max was still staring at Mr Grabber

when his grandfather came to his side. He had just come second in his weightlifting competition – not a bad result for a man as old as he was.

"That's him," he said, following the direction of Max's gaze. "That's Grabber for you – and his son, that little rat, Pablo Grabber." His grandfather paused, and then put an arm around Max's shoulder. "I saw what happened," he said, lowering his voice. "They thought nobody saw, but I did."

"They're cheats," said Max. "They're just a couple of cheats."

"Yes," said Grandfather Gus. "They are. But they seem to get away with it, don't they?"

"One of these days they won't," muttered Max.

"I hope you're right," said Grandfather Gus.

They did not stay for the prize-giving – it would just have been too painful. Pablo Grabber won six races altogether – and he cheated in every one of them. Collecting his trophies, he smiled for the newspaper cameras.

"How do you feel – winning all these trophies?" asked one reporter.

"Pleased," said Pablo. "Mind you, I was expecting to win them."

~ 5 ~

Max tried not to think too much about the Grabbers after that. Just remembering being tripped up in the relay race was enough to make the back of his neck feel warm, and so he decided that the best thing to do was to forget about it. He had learned that lesson from Grandfather Gus, in fact, who had told him that the way to deal with disappointments was to stop dwelling on them. "The more you think about things you don't like," he said, "the more they can get you down. Stop thinking about them, and they go away."

Max had asked him whether he was sure about this, and Grandfather Gus had replied that he was very sure. "Try whistling," he said. "Or try making lists of things you like. That's the way to do it."

It seemed to work, and Max found that he had not given the Grabbers so much as a passing thought, when his mother suddenly announced that she had a big sandwich-making job coming up – and it was at Grabber Mansion.

Grandfather Gus frowned. "I don't like the sound of that," he said. "You shouldn't be making sandwiches for people like that."

Molly laughed. "They won't be eating them themselves. They'll be for their guests. They're having a big party up there."

"I bet their guests will be every bit as nasty as they are," said Grandfather Gus. "Nasty people often have nasty friends. Everybody knows that."

"I can't afford to turn the job down," said Max's mother. "There's not all that much work about these days." She sighed. "Mind you, I don't know how I'm going to manage. They want two thousand sandwiches for all those guests they're

having. Two thousand! How can I be expected to make that many sandwiches, single-handed?"

"Get somebody to help you," said Grandfather Gus. "What about your sister?"

That was Max's Aunt Elsie – an expert

sandwich-maker, known for her fine cheese-and-tomato sandwiches.

"She's already working that day," said Max's mother.

"Or your friend from down the road," suggested Grandfather Gus.

"She's gone off to see her sister," said Molly. "She's going to be away for weeks."

Max had an idea. "What about me?" he volunteered.

Grandfather Gus turned to look at him, with surprise. "You?" he said. "But you already have a job, Max. You cut lawns. You wouldn't have time to make all those sandwiches."

"No, you wouldn't," said his mother. "It's very kind of you to offer, but you have quite enough to do."

Max was determined, and would not take no for an answer. "I have plenty of spare time," he said. "And I really want to help."

"Bless you," said his mother. "But I don't want you to work every hour of the day."

"I don't mind," said Max. "And I really do insist, Mum. You must let me."

Max's mother looked at Grandfather Gus. He hesitated, but then nodded. Turning to her son, she said, "You're the kindest, nicest boy. You really are. And if you insist – which I think you do – then I'll accept."

Max was pleased. "Where will we be making them?" he asked.

"In Grabber Mansion," replied Molly.

"That great big place you pointed out the other day? The one with fountains and statues? That place with all those trees around it?"

"The very place," said Molly. "Exactly the sort of place you'd expect people like that to be living in."

"You be careful," warned Grandfather Gus. "I don't like the thought of my family going there. I don't trust any of those Grabbers."

"We'll be careful," said Max's mother. "You agree, Max?'

Max nodded. "Very careful," he said.

Although the house belonged to the Grabber family, Max felt excited at the thought of going there. He had never been in a house that large, and he wondered how you would find your way around such a vast building. He also wondered whether he would see Pablo Grabber, and whether Pablo would remember him as the boy he had tripped up at the sports day. He might not, of course, because people like Pablo Grabber were always pushing and shoving anybody who got in their way, and could not be expected to remember every time they did it.

Molly had been told to report to Grabber Mansion early on the morning of the party, which would take place at three o'clock in the afternoon. All the supplies for the two thousand sandwiches had been laid out, ready to be loaded into her van, and Max helped to carry these out of the kitchen. There were two hundred loaves of bread, fifty cartons of butter, one thousand tomatoes, four hundred hard-boiled eggs and forty-five jars of strawberry jam. There were other things too, for what Molly called her "speciality sandwiches" – twelve jars of anchovy paste, twenty tins of tuna and over fifty metres of cucumber. It all amounted to a vast pile of food that would soon be transformed by Molly's hard work and skill – and Max's too – into two thousand delicious sandwiches.

As they drove to Grabber Mansion, Molly told Max about the rules of the sandwich-making industry.

"Never cut the bread too thick," she said. "Nor too thin. A thick sandwich tastes too much of bread and too little of the filling. A thin sandwich tastes too much of filling and too little of bread."

Max promised that he would get it just right.

"And don't put too much butter on the bread," Molly went on. "If you use too much butter it oozes out of the edges, and people will get it on their fingers. You have to watch that one."

Max nodded. "I'll be careful," he promised.

"And when you're making tomato sandwiches," Molly said, "make sure that the slices of tomato are not too thick. If they're too thick, they'll make the sandwiches soggy – and that's the worst thing that can happen in this business. If you get a reputation for soggy sandwiches, then you'll soon find yourself with no work at all."

They were now approaching the

turn-off to Grabber Mansion. "There it is," said Max. "There are the gates."

His mother shook her head. "No, they're not for us, Max. Those gates and that driveway are not for the likes of us. We go in the back way – through that gate over there."

She pointed to a much smaller gate some distance away. Max swallowed hard. He glanced at the front gates as they drove past; they were very grand, he thought, with a large coat of arms worked in metal at the top. He could just make out the metal letters at the bottom: *Let Grabber Win*.

"Did you see that?" he said to his mother. "Did you see the motto on the gates?"

"What did it say?"

"It said 'Let Grabber Win'," said Max.

"Shocking," said Molly. "Nobody can win every single time — unless they're selfish and ruthless, the kind who'd sell their own grandmother if it suited them."

Max liked that expression. He could

imagine Pablo Grabber taking his own grandmother to market, with a sign around her neck saying *Grandmother for Sale – Going Cheap*.

"I'd never sell Grandfather Gus," he said. "Not for any amount of money."

"That's the spirit," said Molly. "Money isn't everything, you know, Max. In fact, the really important things in life just can't be bought ..."

"Such as Grandfather Gus?" Max asked.

"Precisely," said Molly.

~ 6 ~

They drove round to the back of the house, where Molly parked the van. Now they had to unload all the sandwich supplies — a task that involved a great deal of fetching and carrying. At last they had everything stacked on a large worktable in the kitchen, ready for the sandwiches — all two thousand of them — to be prepared.

If you've ever made two thousand sandwiches — or even ten, for that matter — you'll know that you have to employ some sort of system. That means that you have to lay out at least twenty slices of bread, and then butter all of them before you start to add the fillings, spreading these over several pieces of bread at the same time, using the largest knife you have. Max soon got the hang of this, and in no time at all he and his mother had made a plateful of sandwiches.

"That's a start," Molly said, smiling at her son. "If we carry on like that, we'll be all right."

They were not the only people working in the kitchen. Although there was no sign of any members of the Grabber family – they thought themselves far too important to stick their noses into the kitchen — their head steward came to inspect progress from time to time. He was an unpleasant-looking man with small, suspicious eyes, and he moved about the kitchen like a shark patrolling a bay. He checked up on the woman who was preparing jug after jug of lemonade; he tasted the cakes being baked in great ovens, by a baker specially brought in for the job; and he picked up a sandwich now and then to make sure it was just right.

Fortunately, the sandwiches met with his approval. "These are good enough," he said. "But don't let me see you slacking! Everything must be perfect by the time the guests arrive."

It was hard work, and Molly could see that Max was getting tired.

"You should take a bit of a break," she said. "I can carry on here while you go outside for a little while. Go on, you deserve it."

Max was pleased to be able to lay aside his breadknife. Slicing loaf after loaf of bread was a demanding task, and his arms were beginning to ache. He looked about him. There were several doors leading out of the kitchen and he could not remember which was the one they had entered through. One of them though looked familiar, and he decided to go through that.

He was wrong. The door he chose did not lead outside, but opened into a long, dimly lit corridor. Max quickly realised his mistake and turned to go back into the kitchen. But now he found, to his alarm, that the door had locked itself behind him and that no matter how he turned the handle, it refused to open.

After trying fruitlessly to open the door, he decided to knock loudly, to attract attention inside the kitchen. This did not work either. Not only was the kitchen a very large room, but there was also a great deal of noise being made by a mixing machine being operated by the baker. This meant that nobody heard his knocking.

There was only one thing to do, and that was to see whether he could find his way outside through any of the other doors further along the corridor.

The first door was no use, as it was firmly locked. He had better luck with the second door though, and he was able to push this open slowly. As he did so, he saw something that made him give a start of surprise. On this door was a sign on which a few words had been painted. It was not a large sign, and it would have been easy to miss it, but Max did see it, and he read out the words under his breath. This is what the sign said: *OTHER PEOPLE'S STUFF*.

Max thought perhaps he had misread the sign, and so he read it out again, just to be sure. It still said the same thing: *OTHER PEOPLE'S STUFF*.

His curiosity firmly aroused, Max opened the door further, so that now he could see

what lay beyond. And it was an extraordin-
ary sight. Max found himself standing in a
room entirely lined with shelves, from
floor to ceiling. A few of these shelves were
empty, but most of them were filled with
objects of every description. He noticed an
old gramophone – one of those ancient
machines with a large brass horn, out of
which the music came. He spotted a pair of
skis and a model boat in a glass case. He
saw several Chinese vases, brightly painted
with scenes of people playing and dancing.
He saw bundles of documents, all tied up
with red tape. There seemed to be something of just about everything you could
ever think of.

Max hesitated. He knew that he should not be in this room, and that if he were found, he would be in trouble. But something told him that he simply had to take a closer look at all these things. And what did that sign mean? Did all these things belong to other people, and, if so, what were they doing stacked up in this room?

And then the answer came to him. It came to him like a light being turned on in the darkness. These things were all stolen goods – everything here was, as the sign made clear, other people's stuff!

Another thought came to him. Was there a chance – just the slightest chance – that if he started to search this room,

he might find the long-lost Ideas Book —
the book of plans that had been taken
by Mr Grabber when he had acquired
Grandfather Gus's factory all those years
ago? The thought made Max's heart beat
faster and faster. Yes. He would look for
it. He would never again get the chance,
and he would not miss it now. He would
search for the book and, if he found it, he
would take it back to Grandfather Gus.
He knew there was a danger that he would
be caught, but he loved his grandfather
and he would take any risk for him — any
risk at all.

~ 7 ~

The trouble was that Max had no idea what the Ideas Book looked like. It was a book, of course – he knew that much – but there was a large number of books on the shelves, and it could have been any of them. So he realised that he would have to work quickly, opening each book to see if any of them looked as if it was a book of plans.

The first ten books he looked at seemed

to be business books, full of figures but not much else. Then there were several books of maps, a couple of ancient dictionaries and even some books with stained covers, full of kitchen recipes. Max looked up at the shelves and sighed. It would take all his time – and all his energy – to work his way along the shelves, but he had to try.

He was rewarded after fifteen minutes, when he reached for an old book with a red cover. Something told him that this was a special book the moment he laid his hands on it, and when he opened the cover and looked at the first page, he knew that he had found what he was looking for. There, in the centre of the page, in large black letters, was his grandfather's name: *AUGUSTUS MONTY CHAMPION*. And underneath, in smaller letters, were the words: *Ideas and Plans for Better Cars*. Finally, at the bottom of the page, came the warning: *Strictly Private*.

Max would have loved to have paged through the Ideas Book, but caution told him that he should not linger in this room of other people's stuff. So, tucking the newly discovered treasure under his arm, he began to make his way towards the door. And it was at this point that he heard voices in the corridor outside.

Max looked about him for places to hide. There was a cupboard on the other side of the room and that, it seemed to him, was the only possible place to conceal himself. The problem though was that he did not know whether there was room for him in this cupboard – it could already be full of other people's stuff – just like the shelves. If that were the case, all would be lost.

To his great relief, the cupboard was largely empty. Climbing inside it, still clutching the book, he pulled the door closed behind him. Now he was in the pitch dark, with only a small crack in the wood to let any light into his cramped and dusty hiding place. Yet in spite of the dark, he felt much safer now; nobody would find him there – unless, of course, somebody chose to look for something in the cupboard ... There was no point in thinking about that possibility though, as there would not be much he could do if that happened. And perhaps the voices he had heard would just go away; perhaps they were the voices of people who were going somewhere else, rather than coming into the Other People's Stuff room.

Unfortunately, they were coming in.

Max heard the door of the room open, and then he heard footsteps and voices, much louder now than they had been before.

"It's somewhere on one of these shelves," said one of the voices. "I think it's up there."

That was a deep voice, and it came from Mr Grabber. It was answered very shortly afterwards by a boy's voice, which Max recognised as the voice of Pablo Grabber. He recognised it because it was the same voice that had boasted about winning the races at the town sports.

"You've got lots of great stuff here, Dad," said Pablo.

"You're right, son," came the reply. And then, after a certain amount of shuffling: "I don't know where it can have got to. It was definitely somewhere here."

"What does it look like?" asked Pablo.

"It's red," said Mr Grabber. "And it has the name of the stupid old man who wrote it on the front page. I hope we find it, son. It's just the thing we need for the competition."

Max was puzzled, but then he remembered something that Grandfather Gus had said about a contest being run to find a better car design. So that must be it: Mr Grabber was planning to steal one of his grandfather's ideas to win the prize. And then he thought, *"The stupid old man"* ... ? Max bristled in anger at those words. Mr Grabber was talking about Grandfather Gus, who was definitely not a stupid old man. How dare these thieves talk about his grandfather like that!

It was at this point, just as Max was struggling to control his feelings of anger at what he had overheard, that he felt a tickle in his nose. It was not a serious tickle to begin with, but slowly it became stronger. It was the dust, of course: if you hide yourself away in a dusty cupboard that has not been opened for months, if not years, then dust is bound to get into your nose, and if dust gets into your nose, you are bound to feel a tickle. And if you feel a tickle in your nose and you cannot do anything about it, then the odds are that you will sneeze.

Max struggled. He took a deep breath in an effort to calm himself, but that only seemed to make it worse. So, next, he breathed out as slowly as he could, but that had the effect of increasing the tick-liness even more. And then, in a gush of relief, he let out the loudest and most cupboard-shaking sneeze of his life. Or that's how it seemed to him – and how it seemed to the wicked Mr Grabber and his unpleasant son, Pablo.

For a few moments, both Grabbers stood quite still. Then Mr Grabber said to his son, "Did you hear that cupboard *sneeze?*"

Pablo Grabber shook his head in wonderment. "I did, Dad, but ... but cupboards can't sneeze, can they?"

"They certainly can't," said Mr Grabber. "But people in cupboards can sneeze, you know."

Inside the cupboard, Max was frozen in dread. Through the little crack in the wood he could now see the two Grabbers advancing slowly towards his hiding place. In terror, he watched as they stopped right in front of the cupboard door. Mr Grabber was scowling, and Pablo Grabber had a cruel grin on his face. They were playing with him; they were deliberately prolonging his fear.

Then Max acted. He did not think it through too much, but he used the one weapon he had in his armoury – surprise.

Throwing the cupboard doors open, he pushed them as hard as he could. Swinging on their hinges, the doors burst open with great force, knocking Pablo Grabber quite off his feet. Down he went on the floor, just as he had made Max fall down on the race track. And as he went down, Mr Grabber, completely taken by surprise, took a step backwards.

This gave Max the chance he needed, and without a moment's delay, he ran across the room to the door that led to the corridor. Pushing this open as quickly as he could, he dashed out and down the corridor, not daring to look behind him, Grandfather Gus's book clutched to his chest as he ran. He heard cries from somewhere behind him, but he paid no attention to them. All that he was thinking of was the need to get as far away as possible from his two Grabber pursuers. He did not care how he did this – all that counted was distance between him and those chasing after him.

There was another door at the end of the corridor, and Max was relieved to discover that this was unlocked. Slipping through it, he found himself at the foot of a wide staircase. He now launched himself up it, taking three, sometimes four, steps at a time. It was a dangerous way to climb a staircase, but Max did not care. It would be far more dangerous to be caught by the pursuing Grabbers.

There was a landing at the top of the stairs, and off this landing there were several open doors. Max saw that these were doors that led to bedrooms, and with a sinking feeling he realised he had run right up into the living quarters of the

Grabber family. This was like running into the very nest of an angry swarm of wasps, or the private cave of a grumpy and cantankerous bear. But there was nowhere else for him to go, and so he ran into the first of these bedrooms, not knowing what to expect, and with no idea of how this would help him evade his would-be captors.

The bedroom belonged to Pablo Grabber. On a dresser near the window, there was a small forest of silver trophies — every one of them, Max thought, the result of a successful bit of cheating. On the walls there were posters of racing cars sponsored by Pablo's father, with *TEAM*

GRABBER painted in large red letters on their sides.

Max looked about him. He wondered whether he might climb out of the window and make his way down by way of a drainpipe. When he looked though, the drop seemed far too long, and he quickly decided that this would be far too perilous. In desperation, he saw that the only possible hiding place was under the bed. It was a tight fit, but he managed it, and did so just in time.

He heard Pablo and his father on the landing.

"He must have gone down the fire escape," said Mr Grabber. "I'm going to go down and have a look."

"He'll have run away by now," said Pablo.

"I'll just check nonetheless," said his father.

"I'll stay up here," said Pablo. "I need to get ready for the party."

Max listened to Mr Grabber's footsteps on the stairs. Then he heard Pablo come into the room; more than that, he was able to see his shoes and ankles as the other boy walked across to the bed. And there Pablo sat down, almost squashing the breath out of Max in his hiding place below.

~ 8 ~

What happened next was one of the oddest, most peculiar, and, looking back on it, one of the most exciting moments of Max's life. Once again, he did not have much time to think about it. Sometimes, the more you think about things, the more reasons you see for not doing whatever it is you were planning.

It was the sight of Pablo's ankles that decided it. They were so close, and they

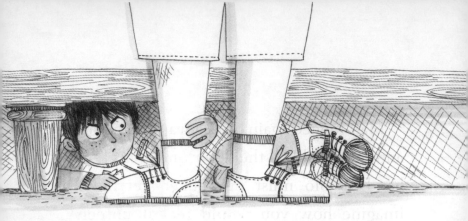

were so fat and tempting, that Max simply had to do what he did. Reaching out with his right hand, he grabbed the ankle closest to him and pulled on it as hard as he could. Up above him, the bed rocked and bucked as the unfortunate boy found one of his legs being dragged away beneath him. At the same time, Pablo began to bawl at the top of his voice. It was a cry of outrage and alarm – a blood-curdling screech.

Max tugged again on the trapped ankle, and then grabbed the other one in his free hand. Pablo must have been terrified: imagine how you would feel if unseen hands suddenly latched on to your ankles and started to tug. He tried to stand up, but this only made matters worse, and he toppled forwards on to the floor of the bedroom, still shouting as loudly as his lungs would permit.

Max now let go, and scooping up his grandfather's book, he scrambled out from under the bed, and flung himself through the door and down the stairs. There was no sign of Pablo coming after him — the other boy was winded and shocked by his fall, and was still trying to get his breath back. But there was every sign of Mr Grabber himself, who, having heard his son's cries, was bounding up the staircase as fast as he could.

They met halfway down the stairs. Max was of course much smaller than Mr Grabber, but he had the advantage of being higher up the staircase. This was enough to make it possible for him to give Mr Grabber a push so powerful that it sent the bully tumbling down the stairs. He was not hurt, but, like his son, he was surprised and confused. This gave Max the time he needed to complete his descent of the staircase and find his way back into the kitchen.

"You've been a long time," said his mother, from behind a growing pile of sandwiches.

"We have to leave," panted Max. "We have to leave right now."

"But we've still got hundreds of sandwiches to make," protested his mother. "It's out of the question."

"But we have to," insisted Max. "I'm being chased by Mr Grabber. If he finds me, we'll both be in trouble."

From behind him came the baker's voice. "That man's chasing you?" he said. "How dare he! He's a brute, that fellow – I've never liked him one little bit."

"He has a room full of stolen stuff," said

Max breathlessly. "A whole room."

The baker looked interested. "That's probably where my recipe books went," he muttered. "They were stolen recently."

Max nodded. "I saw some recipe books," he said. "They might be yours."

The baker growled. "I might have known it." But then he paused. "You said you need to hide?"

"Yes," said Max. "And quickly."

The baker gestured towards a door at the back of the kitchen. "If you go through there," he said, "you'll find yourself in a courtyard. There are lots of storerooms and garages there, and you'll find plenty of places to hide yourself away."

Max did as the baker suggested. There were, as he had been told, plenty of likely looking places to hide, and his eye fell on a set of double doors on which the padlock had been left unlocked. Pushing one of the doors open, he found himself in a large garage, dimly lit by the light from a single high window. As his vision got used to the darkness, he saw that this garage was filled with cars, some of them new and shining, and some of them clearly much older. Many of them had the words *TEAM GRABBER* on their sides, but one simply had the number five on its side.

Max stopped in his tracks. The number five ... And then, in a glorious moment of

recognition, he realised that this was Grandfather Gus's Arabella. So the car had been brought back from India after all — not by Grandfather Gus, of course, but by Mr Grabber. That amounted to theft, thought Max, but then the Grabbers were obviously capable of any amount of theft.

Max was still carrying his grandfather's Ideas Book, and now he had an idea all of his own. He had noticed that the courtyard from which he had entered the garage was on a slope. Not only that, but there was an archway at the bottom end of it that opened on to a steep and winding road running all the way down to the bottom of Mr Grabber's extensive grounds. If he could somehow give Arabella enough of a push to get her going, then he might be able to steer the car out into the courtyard and on to the road. After that, he could find somewhere to hide her, and run off and tell Grandfather Gus of his discovery.

Very gently, Max opened the door of the old car and slipped into the driving seat. Reaching for the handbrake, he pushed it down. The car moved very slightly on the uneven surface of the garage, and Max thought that perhaps it would not be too hard to get it going, if he really tried.

That was what he was thinking when the doors of the garage were suddenly flung open, and there, huffing and puffing and clearly extremely angry, stood Mr Grabber and his son, Pablo.

That was enough for Max. Half-opening the door, he slipped his legs out of the side, and pushed as hard as he could, while the rest of him remained in the driving seat. It was hard work, but as he pushed he felt Arabella begin to roll, slowly at first, and then with gathering speed. When they saw this, Mr Grabber and Pablo both yelled out and lurched towards the car. But Arabella was moving rather quickly now, and they had to jump out of the way to avoid being run over.

"Stop, thief!" shouted Pablo Grabber, waving an indignant fist.

"You're the thieves," muttered Max, as he steered the car out of the garage and into the courtyard. Once there, it was easy. The courtyard sloped sharply, as did the road beyond it, and soon Max was struggling to steer the old car as she shot

down the hill. Looking in the mirror, he saw that the Grabbers were now following him in a large red car. That, he thought, was the Grabber Guzzler, and it made him rather worried. He had only gravity to propel him along, whereas the Grabbers had the powerful engine of the Guzzler. It was an unequal race that they were bound to win, just as they seemed to win everything else.

But there was one thing that the Grabbers did not have on their side, and that was fairness. They had cheated all their lives, but sometimes cheating is not enough to win. And this was one of those times. As the two cars raced down the hill, Max discovered that he had an advantage. The twisting nature of the road made it necessary to brake, but he now discovered that Arabella's brakes no longer worked. That meant that he could not slow down.

The Grabbers, however, did brake, but even then they could not slow down quite enough: as they reached a particularly bad bend, the great, heavy Grabber Guzzler skidded and left the road, plunging into an ornamental lake that Mr Grabber had built further down the hill. There it came to a stop, with Mr Grabber and Pablo stuck out in the middle of the water, in the Guzzler that had now become a large boat. They were powerless to do anything about it, and simply sat on top of the car, fuming and shaking their fists in the direction of the disappearing Arabella.

Max was worried about what would happen at the bottom of the hill. Without brakes, he could not bring the car to a halt, and he was worried that he would hit a

wall or something else solid. At that speed, it would be a very serious accident.

It did not happen. Down at the bottom of the hill, there was a large collection of bushes, and it was into these that Arabella shot like a cannonball. The branches slowed the car down, and when the car eventually stopped altogether, Max realised that he – and Arabella – were largely undamaged.

Unknown to Max, his mother had watched the whole thing from the kitchen window. She had lost no time in calling Grandfather Gus on the phone, telling him to come as quickly as possible to the Grabber estate. So by the time that

Max had pulled himself out of Arabella and found a way through the bushes, Grandfather Gus was already pulling up in his tow truck.

When Grandfather Gus saw Arabella, he gave a cry of joy. "Arabella!" he shouted. "My darling, lovely car!"

It did not take them long to attach a tow rope to Arabella and drag her out of the bushes. Then it was a simple journey back to the garage, where Arabella was safely installed under lock and key, to prevent the Grabbers from stealing her again.

When Molly came back later that day, she and Grandfather Gus heard the full story from Max. Grandfather Gus was very interested to hear about the conversation Max had overheard between Mr Grabber and his son. "I might just enter that competition myself," he mused. "Now that I have my Ideas Book back, I can take another look at some of those plans."

Max offered to help, and over the next few weeks he and Grandfather Gus were kept busy, making the parts that would be installed in Arabella for the competition. At the end, when they had put in the last few nuts and bolts, the old car was completely transformed and ready for the competition.

Did Arabella win? Of course she did. And that made the Grabbers furious, but there was nothing they could do. They had learned that cheating never pays, in the end.

Now that Arabella was back on the road, many people saw her and asked Grandfather Gus to make them cars just like her.

He was happy to do this, as he'd spent the money he received as his competition prize on some very efficient new machinery. That kept him busy, of course, but not too busy to take Max and his mother for regular rides in Arabella. He also promised Max that before long he would enter Arabella in another rally — not to India this time, but still an exciting one — and Max could come along as navigator.

"And who knows," said Grandfather Gus, "in a few years' time, when you're older, you might become a rally driver yourself."

Max smiled. Anything, he thought, was possible.

Max, Molly and Grandfather Gus were all very happy with the way things had worked out. As for the Grabbers, they learned their lesson. As the popularity of Grandfather Gus's cars grew, there were very few people who wanted to buy a Grabber Guzzler. This meant that the Grabbers soon found they had very little money. They had to sell their mansion, which was turned into a sports centre for people in the neighbourhood, and they went to live in a small house on the edge of town. They discovered that it was far better to live modestly and honestly than to be dishonest and live in a great big mansion.

Pablo Grabber stopped cheating and even became a friend to Max, who let him help clean cars on Saturday mornings.

The two boys sometimes went to the cinema together after they had finished at the garage, and Max always shared his popcorn with Pablo, who thanked him and never took more than his fair share.

As for Max's mother, Molly, her life took a turn for the better when Grandfather Gus invented a sandwich-making machine for her. This worked very well and made her job a whole lot easier.

"We're very lucky to have you," said Molly to Grandfather Gus, as she tried out the new machine.

"Yes," said Max. "We're very lucky."

"And I'm lucky to have *you*," said Grandfather Gus, with a smile.

RUN AWAY TO THE CIRCUS!

Read on for a sneak peek
at Freddie's lion-sized adventure

AVAILABLE NOW!

~ 5 ~

His heart beating hard within him, Freddie poked his head round the flap of canvas at the main entrance to the big tent. It was dark inside, apart from a pool of light around the ring.

"Freddie!" called out a voice from the darkness. He recognised it as Lisa's.

And then another voice came from somewhere up above. "Lisa will help you up." That was Godfrey.

Freddie advanced slowly towards the ring. As he did so, Lisa emerged from the shadows. She was wearing the sparkling costume he had seen at the show.

"Here," she said, handing Freddie an outfit made of the same spangled material. "This should fit you. You can change in the ticket booth."

Freddie did as he was told, donning the unfamiliar costume. It felt very strange to be wearing something like that when he had no idea at all of how to use a trapeze. But, once changed, he went back to the ring and stood, shivering ever so slightly, at Lisa's side.

"Don't be nervous," she said. "It looks

very dangerous but it's really completely safe. The net, you see, will catch you if you fall. You'll just bounce."

Freddie cast his eyes upwards. "Are you sure?"

Lisa laughed. "Of course I'm sure." She took him by the hand and led him to a rope ladder. "Look, let me show you. We'll climb to that platform up there – where the trapeze is – and then I'll let go and fall. You'll see how the safety net works. Then you can do the same."

Freddie gasped. "Fall?" he asked.

"Yes," she said. "It's very simple. Just let go of the trapeze and see what happens. You'll fall, of course, but you'll land in the net and bounce up. It's great fun, you know."

For a few moments Freddie toyed with the idea of running away. If he turned on his heels and ran, then he could just carry on running until he came to the main road. He could catch a bus there and be home in no time at all. But if he did that, then it would be the end of his job at the circus, and he was so looking forward to his wages . . .

Then he thought of his mother, working so hard for such long hours on those distant ships. She had to do things that she did not want to do — she would far rather be at home, he thought — and yet she never complained. If she could do that for the good of the family, then the least he could do was to try to earn a little bit of money. And if that meant that he had to swing on a trapeze, then that was what he would do.

He turned to Lisa. "I'm ready," he said.

She smiled encouragingly. "Good," she said. "Then let's start climbing."

It did not take long to reach the platform up at the top. Godfrey was waiting for them there, holding on to a trapeze with one hand while he used the other to help them onto the platform.

"Freddie is going to have a bit of practice with the net," said Lisa. "I'll go first."

"Righty-ho," said Godfrey, passing the trapeze to her. "Here you are."

Lisa placed both her hands on the trapeze. "I'm just going to swing a few times," she explained to Freddie. "Then I'll let go and fall. Watch me hit the net down below and bounce back. It's quite simple, you know – nothing to it!"

Turning around, she bent her knees and launched herself off the edge of the platform.

"There she goes," said Godfrey. "Swinging nicely, just like . . ." He suddenly stopped, and Freddie knew immediately that something was wrong.